3CESL000027157

W9-BRX-628

Zeely Zebra

Barbara deRubertis
Illustrated by Eva Vagreti Cockrille

The Kane Press
New York

Cover Design: Sheryl Kagen

Copyright © 1997 by The Kane Press
All rights reserved. No part of this book may be reproduced or transmitted in any
form or by any means, electronic or mechanical, including photocopying
recording, or by any information storage and retrieval system, without permission
in writing from the publisher. For information regarding permission, write to
The Kane Press, 240 West 35th Street, Suite 300, New York, NY 10001-2506.

Library of Congress Cataloging-in-Publication Data

DeRubertis, Barbara.
Zeely Zebra/Barbara deRubertis; illustrated by Eva Vagreti Cockrille.
p.   cm.
"A Let's read together book."

Summary: Although she is not the biggest or strongest or fastest zebra, Zeely
practices very hard, with the help of Speedy Cheetah, and wins a spot on the Zebra
All Star Racing Team.
ISBN 1-57565-023-1 (pbk. : alk. paper)
[1. Zebras--Fiction. 2. Racing--Fiction. 3. Stories in rhyme.]
I. Vagreti Cockrille, Eva, ill.   II. Title.
PZ8.3.D455Ze 1997   96-52644
[E]--dc21   CIP
                                         AC

10 9 8 7 6 5

First published in the United States of America in 1997 by The Kane Press.
Printed in China.

LET'S READ TOGETHER is a registered trademark of The Kane Press.

Zeely Zebra
is so sweet—
the sweetest zebra
you will meet.

But for a zebra,
Zeely's small.
She is not big.
She is not tall.

She is not strong.
She is not fast.
In races, Zeely
comes in last.

But Zeely has a
secret dream
of being on the
racing team.

She wants to run
the tryout race.
She wants to win—
to take first place.

Then she will reach
her secret dream!
She'll make the All Star
Racing Team!

9

But Zeely knows
she can't just dream.
She must work hard
to make the team.

"I must get help
without delay.
And I must practice
every day.

"Who will teach me?
Speedy will!
Speedy Cheetah
fills the bill!"

Zeely Zebra
squeaks with glee.
"Speedy's sleeping
by the tree!"

Zeely leans down
on her knees.
"Speedy, help me!
Please! Oh, please!

"Teach me how to
run like you.
Help me make my
dream come true."

Slowly, Speedy
starts to speak.
"First we'll leap
across the creek."

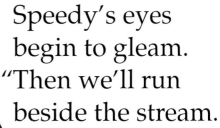

Speedy's eyes
begin to gleam.
"Then we'll run
beside the stream.

"Every day I'll
meet you here.
I will teach you!
Never fear."

For weeks and weeks
the two friends meet.
And Zeely runs
in steamy heat.

Zeely runs
in freezing rain—
across the green
and grassy plain.

21

She beats her feet
between the trees.
Now she's running
like the breeze.

Speedy speaks
with beaming face.
"You are ready
for the race!"

"On your mark..."
   says the speaker.
   Zeely Zebra
   sets her sneaker.

"Get...set..."
   the speaker screeches.
   Zeely leans.
   Zeely reaches.

THE ZEBRA
ALL
STAR
RACING TEAM

"Now...GO!"
the speaker screams.

Zeely Zebra
puffs and steams.

Across the creek,
Zeely leaps.

Beside the stream,
Zeely sweeps.

Speedy Cheetah
cheers for Zeely.
"You can do it,
Zeely! Really!"

Hear the screaming!
Hear the cheering!
Now the finish
line is nearing!

Zeely wins!
See Speedy beam!
And Zeely Zebra
makes the team!

Let's cheer three cheers!
Hip, hip, hooray!
Hard work and dreams
have made the day!